This book belongs to:

. . . .

To my beautiful Lottie, for all the steps she's taken and all the steps to come. A.S.

This book is dedicated to Aslom for his work with children, and to Jaime's admiration for him. L.M.

First edition for North America published in 2011
by Barron's Educational Series, Inc.

Original edition published by Oxford University Press 2010

This book was designed and produced by
Oxford University Press
Great Clarendon Street, Oxford 0X2 6DP
Great Britain

Database right Oxford University Press (maker)

All inquiries should be addressed to:
Barron's Educational Series, Inc.
250 Wireless Boulevard
Hauppauge, NY 11788
www.barronseduc.com

ISBN: 978-0-7641-4683-1

Library of Congress Control Number: 2010937035

Date of Manufacture: April 2011
Manufactured by: Prosperous Printing,
Shen Zhen, China

Printed in China
9 8 7 6 5 4 3 2 1

Amber Stewart & Layn Marlow

Puddle's New School

BARRON'S

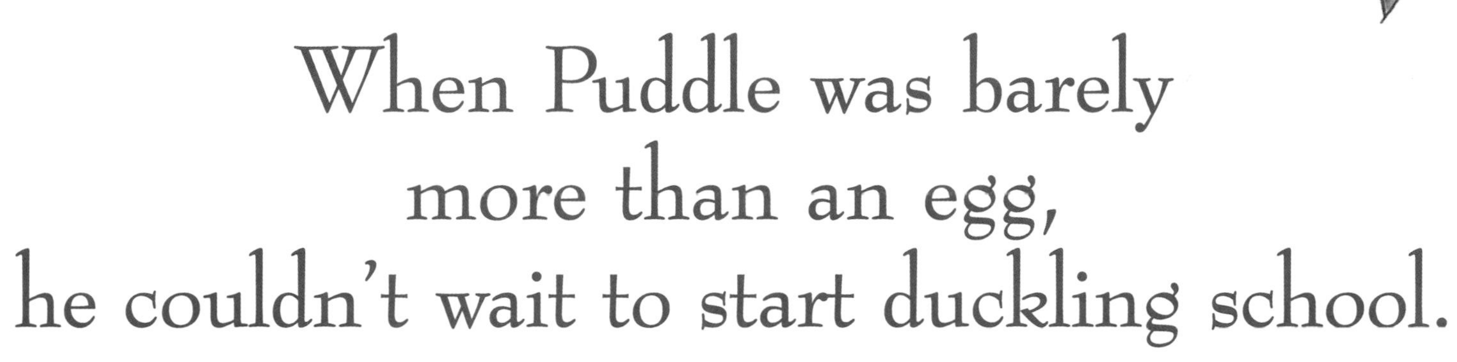

When Puddle was barely
more than an egg,
he couldn't wait to start duckling school.

Every day, Puddle and his two friends, Pip and Fern, would watch the bigger ducklings waddling to and from Willow Brook Duckling School.

They looked so grown-up —
each with their own school bag . . .

and Puddle wished
to be just like them.

Then, one day, while Puddle was helping
Mommy to make his favorite biscuits,
Mommy gave him a big hug and said,
"Puddle, now *you* are big enough
to start duckling school."

Puddle's feathers fluffed out with pride.

"Will I have my very own
school bag, Mommy?"
he asked.

"Yes you will,"
Mommy smiled.
"Your own special bag."

But tucked up in their nest that night,
Puddle imagined his first day at school and
his little heart went pitter-patter, pitter-patter.

As he edged just a bit closer to Mommy's warm, soft feathers, Puddle knew that he'd been wrong. He *could* wait to go to duckling school . . .

he could wait until he was a very big duck indeed.

"Every new little duckling at Willow Brook will feel wobbly today," Mommy said kindly, slipping Puddle's bag over his wing.

"Your first day at school is a very big step."

But Puddle wasn't sure he could take even

one

very

small

step.

His feet
felt stuck to
the ground.

"You'll have fun," smiled Mommy,
as she shooed him gently along the
stepping-stones into school.
"You're my brave little duck."

As Puddle put down his school bag, he spotted something . . . something very familiar.

It was one of Mommy's smallest, softest feathers. She had tucked it inside to show she was never far away.

Then Puddle felt brave enough
to take his next big step . . .

and found a place to sit on the water-lily mat.
"I like your feather," whispered the little
duck beside him.

The morning went by in a flurry of . . .

matching
ladybugs . . .

counting
caterpillars . . .

and lily-pad leaping . . .

until their teacher clapped
her wings and asked them
all to settle down for lunch.

Puddle and Mommy had lunch together every day.
Suddenly, she did seem very far away.

But when Puddle took his lunch box from his special bag, he found Mommy had packed all his favorite snacks . . .

and four of the best home-made biscuits — one for him, one for Pip, one for Fern, and one for a new friend, too.

After lunch, it was nap time
under the willow tree.

Puddle peeked in his bag,
hoping that Mommy had
remembered his Blankie . . .

and she had.

Later, all the ducklings made presents for their mommies and daddies.

Some made feet paintings,

some made daisy chains,

and some decorated twigs.

When it was time to go home,
Puddle tucked his twig carefully
into his bag, and ran happily along
the stepping-stones for a warm,
soft hug from Mommy.

Snuggled up in their nest that night,
Puddle thought about his first day at school
and his little heart went pitter-patter,
pitter-patter with excitement . . .

he couldn't wait to see
what he would do tomorrow
at duckling school.